Only Fish Fall from the Sky

Published in North America by POW!
a division of powerHouse Packaging & Supply, Inc.

Text and illustrations © 2015 Leif Parsons

ISBN 978-157687-757-9

Library of Congress Control Number: 2014948106

powerHouse Packaging & Supply, Inc.
37 Main Street, Brooklyn, NY 11201-1021

info@powkidsbooks.com
www.powkidsbooks.com
www.powerHousebooks.com
www.powerHousepackaging.com

First edition, 2015

10 9 8 7 6 5 4 3 2 1

Printed in Malaysia

Only Fish Fall From The Sky
Leif Parsons

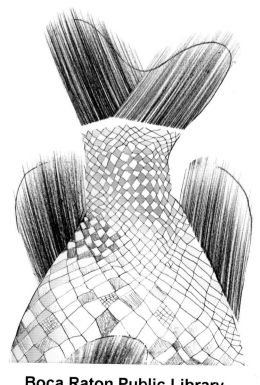

When I woke up I remembered
I had the strangest **dream.**

I dreamt that water fell from the sky.

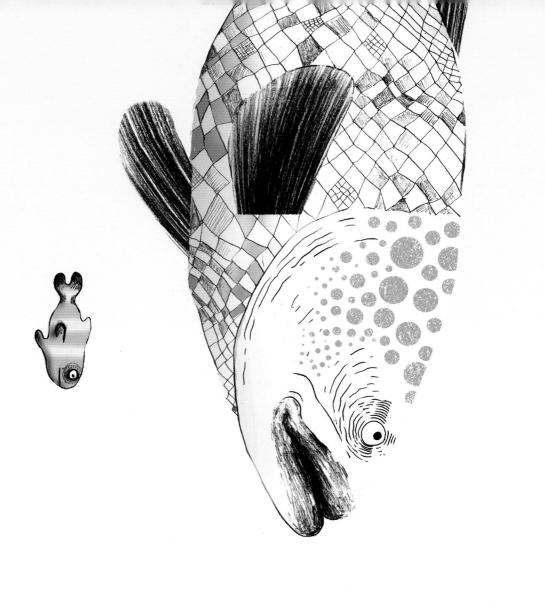

How ridiculous.

Everyone knows only fish fall from the sky.

In my **dream**, everything was right-side up.
As I walked to school, I thought,

Wouldn't that be wonderful?
I could get everywhere so quickly!

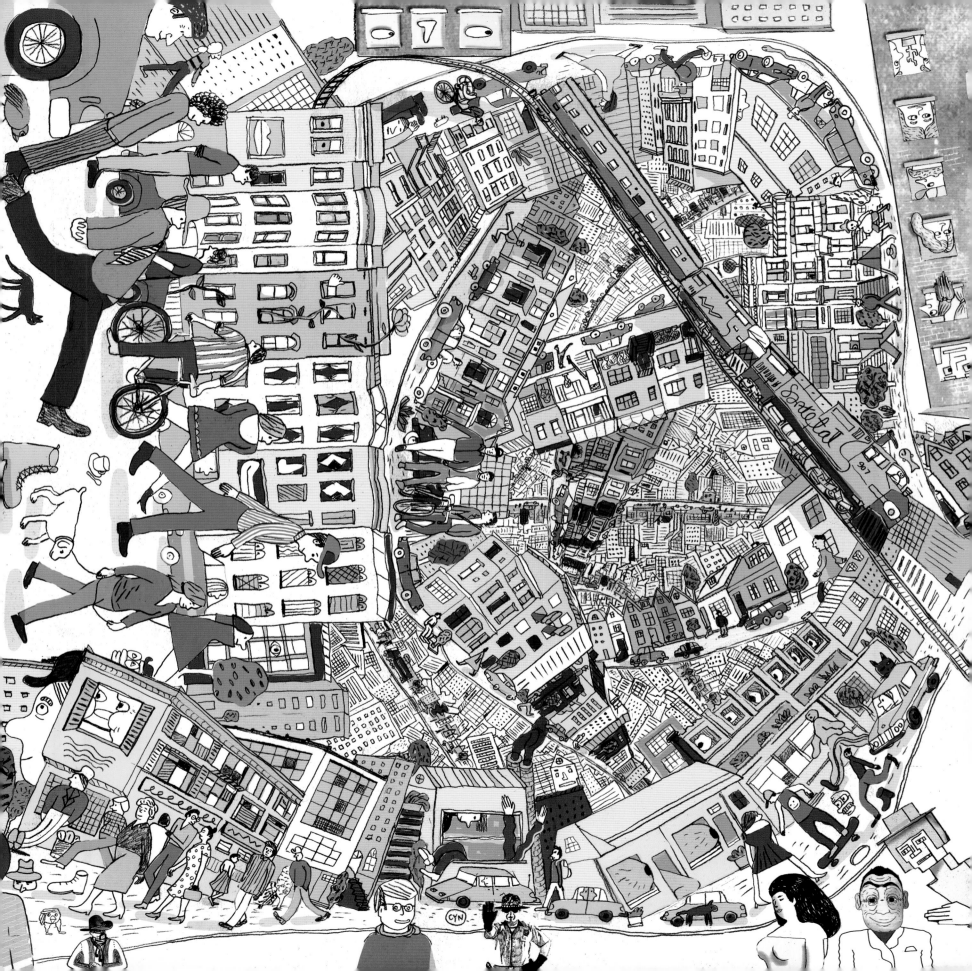

In my dream,
only children came to class.

When I sat down, I thought,
preposterous!

Why wouldn't everyone
want to go to school?

In my dream
we played in a schoolyard.

When we went outside,
I thought, what a crazy idea,

wouldn't they
miss the view?

In my dream,
people ate meals sitting down.

When I got home, I thought,
How rude!

Everyone knows,
it is only polite to dance at dinner.

In my dream,
everyone slept in a bed.

As I curled up, I thought,
wouldn't that be odd?

I certainly would
miss the company.

When I woke up I remembered
I had the strangest dream.

I dreamt that fish fell from the sky!

E
Parsons, Leif,
Only fish fall from the sky /

Jun 2015